My Adventures With

Disney
FROZEN
FEVER

This book was especially written for
Emily Nicholson

Adapted by Kate Andresen

ISBN 978-1-875676-58-3

In Arendelle, Queen Elsa was planning a surprise birthday party for her little sister. Anna had never had a real birthday, so Elsa wanted it to be a memorable occasion.

A beautifully decorated birthday cake stood in the middle of the courtyard. It was up to Elsa to create a perfect topping for the cake.

Emily Nicholson was at home celebrating a special day—it was Emily's birthday!

A birthday cake was decorated with little statues of Elsa, Anna, Olaf, Kristoff and Sven from Emily's favorite movie *Frozen*. Inscribed around the base of the cake were the words 'Happy Birthday Emily!'

Eyes closed, Emily blew out the candles and made a wish.

In Arendelle, the birthday preparations were well underway. The courtyard was filled with balloons and streamers and there was a vase with bright flowers on each table.

Sven helped Kristoff paint a birthday banner with Anna's name on it. The letters were strung together and hung on a rope that stretched across the entire courtyard.

Often, Emily imagined visiting Arendelle. Emily was happy to see that Elsa, Anna and the entire kingdom were much happier now.

Emily really wanted to go back as it was Anna's birthday today, too. While dreaming, Emily returned to Arendelle and found Elsa, Kristoff and Sven in the courtyard.

"It's Anna's birthday and we're planning a surprise party. We could do with some help, Emily," said Elsa.

Emily was delighted.

Elsa left Kristoff in charge while she and Emily went to wake the birthday girl.

They tiptoed into Anna's room and Elsa gently woke her sister. "It's time to wake up, Anna. It's your birthday and it's going to be perfect!"

"Happy birthday, Anna!" cried Emily.

"Emily! What a wonderful surprise!" replied Anna.

Elsa presented Anna with a new dress. Anna gasped with delight when she saw her beautiful teal skirt embroidered with bright yellow sunflowers. "I love it!" Anna cried, twirling.

Then Elsa handed Emily a beautiful green dress with tiny flowers sewn on the hemline.

Emily was overjoyed. "Thank you, Elsa, it's beautiful!"

With a magical flourish, Elsa created a new dress for herself, too!

Elsa had hidden lots of gifts for Anna throughout the kingdom. She held up a piece of string and handed it to Anna.

"Just follow the string!" smiled Elsa.

Elsa and Emily laughed as they watched Anna crawl under a large chair and over a small table. The string kept going from room to room!

Finally, the birthday string led them out of the castle and down to the docks by the fjord. There, they found a rowboat, and next to the rowboat, Anna spotted her next present. "A fishing pole!" she exclaimed.

"Achoo!" Elsa sneezed. As she did, a flurry of little snowgies appeared behind her.

"Are you all right, Elsa?" asked Emily.

They didn't notice the little snowgies scampering away.

In the courtyard, Kristoff and Sven were working hard to get everything ready for Anna's big birthday bash.

Kristoff was surprised to see a group of little snowgies appear. Every time he turned around, there were more of them.

Olaf was thrilled. "Little brothers!" he squealed happily.

Kristoff was getting worried. More and more little snowgies arrived. They climbed onto the tables and skidded across the tablecloths, knocking over flower arrangements.

When they started climbing up to the cake, Kristoff knew he had to act. He grabbed Olaf's head off his body and rolled it like a bowling ball. Olaf knocked down the pyramid of little snowgies!

Meanwhile, Elsa led Anna and Emily to the square where a group of schoolchildren were gathering. Elsa stood in front of them and raised her hands. The children started singing a song that had been written specially for Anna's birthday.

Elsa sneezed again. More little snowgies appeared, landing right on the stage with the choir. The snowgies ran around the stage, causing great excitement!

In the courtyard, the snowgies were creating chaos. Some of them pulled down the birthday banner. As Kristoff was still busy protecting the cake, Olaf decided that he would fix the banner.

When Olaf had finished, Kristoff stared at the newly rearranged letters which read "DRY BANANA HIPPY HAT".

"Oh, no! I wish Emily was here to help us!" exclaimed Kristoff.

It wasn't Olaf's fault that he couldn't read or spell!

Elsa's nose was stuffy and she couldn't stop sneezing, but she was too excited to end the treasure hunt now.

She led Anna and Emily to the bottom of Arendelle's clock tower. "Come on. Up we go," she told them.

Anna was starting to worry about her sister, but there didn't seem to be any way to stop Elsa's excitement.

They climbed to the top of the clock tower.

They reached the top of the stairs and Elsa led Anna and Emily
through a door that opened onto a ledge in front of the giant clock face.

There they found two wooden dolls that looked just like Anna and Elsa!

As they stood on the ledge, Elsa twirled, trying to make a flourish… but she lost her balance and started to fall. Anna rushed to her side. Elsa was burning up with fever.

Anna and Emily helped Elsa back down the clock tower. When they reached the castle, Anna leaned her back against the gates to open them.

Behind Anna, Elsa and Emily could see hundreds of little snowgies! Olaf, Sven and Kristoff were tossing the cake back and forth to keep it away from the curious snowgies.

As the snowgies jumped at the cake, Kristoff grabbed it and
scrambled onto Sven's shoulders, holding the cake high above his head.

Anna turned to see what Elsa and Emily were looking at.

At that moment, everyone froze. The birthday banner fluttered back into place. Somehow it spelled out the correct message: "HAPPY BIRTHDAY ANNA".

Anna was thrilled.

Kristoff carried the cake toward Anna singing, *"Happy birthday, Anna, I love you!"*

Anna knew her sister needed to rest. "To bed with you, Elsa," she insisted.

Anna and Emily finally put Elsa to bed. "Best birthday present ever, you know," Anna said.

Elsa thought for a second. "Which one?"

"You letting me take care of you," replied Anna.

Emily sat quietly, reflecting on a truly memorable day. Emily fell asleep, but was soon woken by singing.

'Happy birthday to you. Happy birthday dear Emily, happy birthday to you,' Emily's family and friends were singing.

Emily was back home, and the birthday party had begun!

High up on the North Mountain, Marshmallow heard a knock on the front door.

"Hi, Marshmallow!" Olaf exclaimed. "Did you miss me?"

And with that, Olaf, Kristoff and Sven breezed into the palace… followed by hundreds of little snowgies.

"You're going to love this place!" Olaf told the little snowgies.

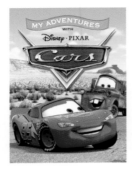

This personalized Disney Frozen Fever book was especially created for Emily Nicholson.

If Emily loved starring in this personalized My Adventure Book then there are many more exciting stories available.

Visit us at www.putmeinthestory.com

Contact us at support@putmeinthestory.com

Our return address for shipping is:
1935 Brookdale Road, Suite 139
Naperville, IL 60563

1111 001438 0001 01 DS 0094